Boots

and

His Brothers

A Norwegian Tale retold
by Eric A. Kimmel

Illustrated by Kimberly Bulcken Root

Holiday House/New York

For Elin, Anders, and Annika
E.A.K.

For my brother Kent, ''Boots''
K.B.R.

Library of Congress Cataloging-in-Publication Data
Kimmel, Eric A.
Boots and his brothers : a Norwegian tale / retold by
Eric A. Kimmel : illustrations by Kimberly Bulcken Root.—1st ed.
p. cm.
Summary: A young man's kindness to an old beggar woman earns him
his weight in gold and half a kingdom.
ISBN 0-8234-0886-8
[1. Folklore—Norway.] I. Root, Kimberly Bulcken, ill.
II. Title.
PZ8.1.K567Bo 1991   90-23659   CIP   AC
398.2—dc20
[E]

I've been telling the story of "Boots and His Brothers" for nearly fifteen years. The version I tell is adapted from one in Edgar and Ingri Parin D'Aulaire's *East of the Sun and West of the Moon*. The standard collection of Norwegian stories is, of course, Asbjørnsen and Moe's *Norwegian Fairy Tales*.

Some changes have crept into the story since I began telling it. In the original version, Peter and Paul have their heads chopped off. I prefer to let the dogs chase them. The ax and spade were once full-size until I came upon a dollhouse shop that sold tiny tools. I was able to buy a wonderful ax and spade that fit into the palm of my hand. Now, whenever I tell the story, I reach into my pocket, and there they are. Hack and hew, dig and delve away!

The story probably has roots in the coming of Christianity to Scandinavia. Gigantic oak trees were sacred to the ancient Norsemen. The first missionaries lost no time in cutting them down.

ERIC A. KIMMEL
June 15, 1991

Once upon a time three brothers set out to seek their fortune. The first was Peter. He was rough and rude. The second was Paul. He was rude and rough. The third was Boots. He wasn't rough or rude at all. He got his name from a pair of tall boots that he always wore.

One day, as Peter, Paul, and Boots walked along the road, they encountered a beggar woman.

"Where are you going, young gentlemen?" the beggar woman asked.

"We are bound to seek our fortune, if it's any business of yours," Peter answered.

"Then you are in luck, for your fortune lies only three days' journey away." She pointed with her stick. "In that direction lies a mountain. At the top of the mountain is a castle, and in the castle lives a king. A great oak tree blocks the light from his windows. He has promised to pay his weight in gold to anyone who can chop down that tree. He would also like someone to dig a well and fill it with sweet water, for there is no source of sweet water anywhere on the mountain."

"Peter and I could do that in an afternoon," Paul exclaimed. "What are we waiting for? Let's go!"

The beggar woman held out her hand. "Kind gentlemen, if I have helped you, perhaps you could help me."

"Why should we give you anything, old witch? You've already told us all we need to know," Peter said, pushing her aside as he ran to catch up with Paul. Boots remained behind. He pressed a coin into the beggar woman's hand.

"Excuse my brothers, Granny. They are not as bad as they seem."

"I daresay they are worse," the beggar woman muttered. "But you are not at all like them. Therefore I will tell you something useful. It is not easy to win your weight in gold.

A magic spell hangs over the oak tree. For every chip that is chopped, two chips grow in its place. Digging the well and filling it with water are just as difficult. The castle lies on top of an iron mountain. No pickax can cut it; no shovel can dig it. The nearest source of sweet water is a hundred leagues away. Many have attempted these tasks. All have failed. When they do, the king sets his dogs on them."

Boots scratched his head. "Can these things be done at all?"

"You can do them, if you follow this advice. Whenever

you ask a question, do not rest until you find the answer."

"That is good advice in any case," said Boots, slipping another coin into the woman's hand. "Wish me luck, Granny!" And down the road he ran to join his brothers.

They walked the rest of that day. By late afternoon they sat down by the roadside to rest. As they sat they heard a chop-chop-chopping sound.

"I wonder what's making that noise?" Boots asked.

Peter and Paul laughed at him. "Don't be a ninny! Everyone knows what that is. It's the sound of an ax chopping trees."

But Boots remembered the old woman's advice. "I have asked a question. Now I must find the answer."

"Don't be too long about it," Peter and Paul grumbled as Boots walked off into the forest.

In a little while he came upon a clearing where tall trees lay tumbled over each other like jackstraws. A tiny ax no bigger than a child's forefinger flew through the air, cutting down trees with one stroke. Surprised, Boots exclaimed, "Why, there you are, hacking and hewing!"

To his greater surprise the ax answered, "I hack and hew the livelong day, waiting for you."

"Well, here I am," Boots said. He caught the ax by the handle and slipped it into his knapsack. Then he went back to join his brothers.

"What did you find?" Peter and Paul asked when he returned.

"Oh, you were right," Boots said. "It was only an ax chopping down trees." But he didn't tell them the rest.

They traveled a second day. At noon they stopped beside the road to eat. As they sat they heard a dig-dig-digging sound.

"I wonder what's making that noise?" asked Boots.

"Don't be a dunce!" said Peter and Paul. "Everyone knows what that is. It's the sound of a spade digging a hole."

But Boots remembered the old woman's advice. "I have asked a question. Now I must find the answer."

"Don't be too long about it," Peter and Paul grumbled as Boots walked off into the forest.

In a little while he came upon a deep pit from which spadefuls of earth flew in a steady stream. Boots leaned over the edge of the pit and looked down. At the bottom he saw a tiny spade no bigger than a child's thumb digging up the ground and making the dirt fly.

"Why there you are, digging and delving!" Boots exclaimed.

The spade answered, "I dig and delve the livelong day, waiting for you."

"Well, here I am," Boots said. He reached into the pit, caught the spade, and slipped it into his knapsack. Then he went back to join his brothers.

"What did you find?" Peter and Paul asked when he returned.

"Oh, you were right," Boots said. "It was only a spade digging a hole." But he didn't tell them the rest.

By the end of the third day the three brothers, tired and footsore, stopped to rest beside a rushing, rippling stream. As they soaked their feet in the cool water, Boots remarked, "I wonder where this stream comes from?"

"Don't be a goose!" Peter and Paul told him. "This stream comes from the same place every other stream comes from."

"Where is that?"

"From a hole!"

But Boots remembered the old woman's advice. "I have asked a question. Now I must find the answer."

"Don't be too long about it," Peter and Paul grumbled as Boots followed the stream into the forest.

The stream grew smaller and smaller until it was no thicker than a piece of string. Boots followed it all the way to a rocky ledge. A walnut rested on the ledge. The stream flowed out of a hole in the walnut's side.

"Why there you are, rushing and rippling!" Boots exclaimed.

"Yes," the walnut replied, "I rush and ripple the livelong day, waiting for you."

"Well, here I am," said Boots. He plugged the hole with a bit of moss and slipped the walnut into his knapsack. Then he went back to join his brothers.

"Did you find where the stream comes from?" Peter and Paul asked when he returned.

"Oh, you were right," Boots said. "It comes out of a hole." But he didn't tell them the rest.

The next day they arrived at the castle. "I'm oldest, so I'll go first," Peter said. He walked right up to the gate and knocked boldly, ignoring the pack of ferocious dogs tied up outside.

The king looked out the window. "What do you want?"

"Give me my weight in gold," Peter answered, none too politely.

"Chop down the oak tree first," the king commanded.

Peter stared at the enormous tree. Its trunk was as thick as a threshing floor. Its branches blotted out the sun. Peter picked up the ax that lay beside it and gave the tree a mighty chop. A mighty chip flew, but two equally mighty chips grew in its place. Peter began chopping frantically, but the faster he chopped, the thicker the tree grew.

"Enough!" the king cried to his servants. "He's tried and failed. Set the dogs on him!" The servants loosed two of the dogs who chased Peter down the mountain and out of sight.

"I'm next," said Paul.

He was much stronger than Peter. He gave the oak a tremendous chop. A tremendous chip flew, but two equally tremendous chips grew in its place. Paul began chopping frantically, but the tree only grew thicker.

"Enough!" the king cried. "Set the dogs on him." The servants loosed two more dogs who chased Paul down the mountain and over the next hill.

"May I try, Your Majesty?" Boots asked. The dogs at the gate wagged their tails when he came forward.

The king looked glum. "Go ahead if you like. Many have tried, but the tree only gets thicker. I am beginning to think that no one can cut it down. My castle will never see sunlight again."

"Oh yes it will!" said Boots. He reached into his knapsack and took out the tiny ax. "Hack and hew away!"

The tiny ax whirled through the air. It cleaved the tree with a single stroke. The great oak tottered. Then, with a thunderous crack, it came crashing down. Sunlight streamed through the castle windows for the first time in years. The king was overjoyed.

"Young man, you have earned your weight in gold," he said to Boots. "Now if you can only dig a well in this iron mountain and fill it with sweet water, you can have half my kingdom now and the other half when I am dead."

"I am happy to serve," Boots answered. He reached into his knapsack, took out the tiny spade, and, placing it on the ground, cried, "Dig and delve away!"

The spade made the iron rocks fly. In no time at all it had dug a well deep into the mountainside.

"Excellent," said the king, looking down into the hole. "But how will you fill a well that deep with water?"

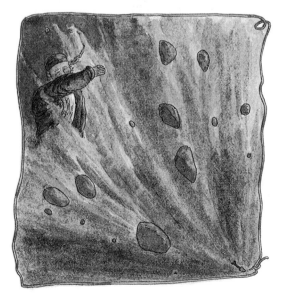

"No trouble at all," said Boots. He reached into his knapsack and took out the walnut. Removing the moss plug, he dropped the walnut into the well. "Rush and ripple away!"

A rushing, rippling stream came gurgling out of the walnut, filling the well with an unending flow of pure, sweet water. Everyone in the castle applauded.

"You have accomplished all three tasks," the king said.
"You may now claim your reward."

"I would like something for my brothers too," Boots said.
The king replied, "They can be dogkeepers."

Thus it was that Boots won his weight in gold and half a kingdom. When the old king died, Boots became king in his place. And a very good king he was, too.